Munich

STORYTELLER'S NOTE

The French legend of the little juggler who
offers the gift of his talent and the miracle
that occurs is well known. The version
I loved as a child was the one told by the
master storyteller Anatole France. In
the oral tradition, storytellers through the
centuries have told and retold tales,
changing them often to fit their own lives
and mores. Following this tradition, I have
lovingly retold this ancient legend, shaping
it to my own life and experience, and
called it by its oldest known title.

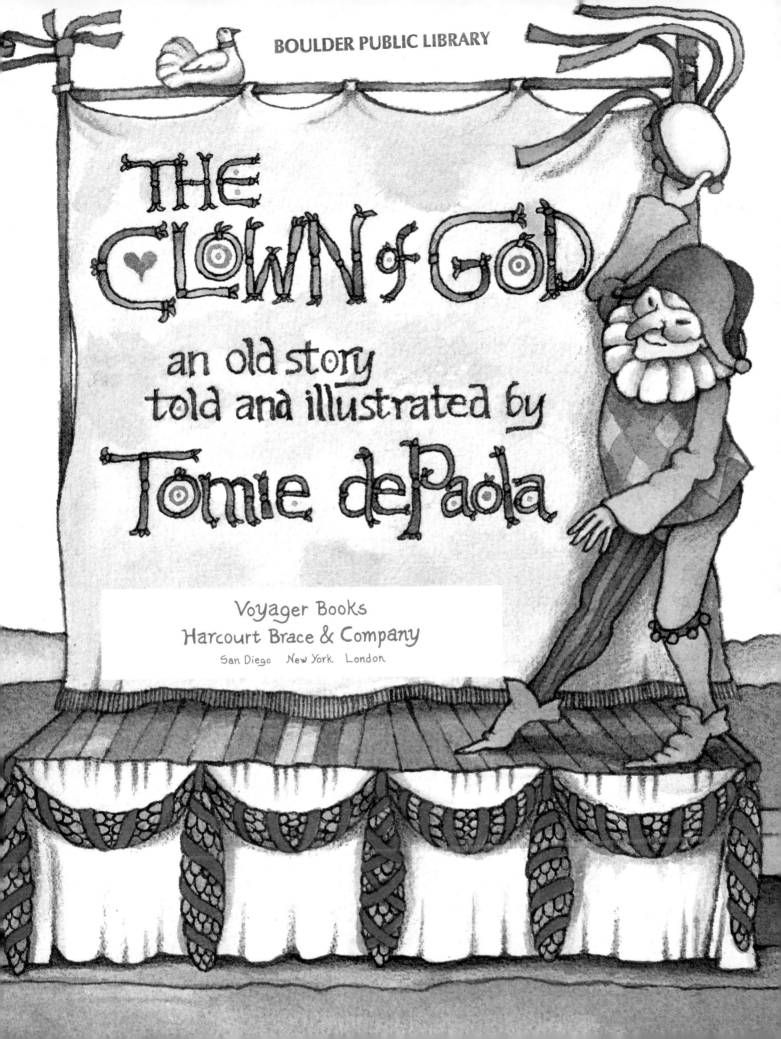

THE CLOWN of GOD

an old story
told and illustrated by

Tomie dePaola

Voyager Books
Harcourt Brace & Company
San Diego   New York   London

for
Norine Odland

Requests for permission to make copies of any part of the
work should be mailed to: Permissions Department,
Harcourt Brace & Company, 6277 Sea Harbor Drive,
Orlando, Florida 32887-6777.

Voyager Books is a registered trademark of
Harcourt Brace & Company.

Library of Congress Cataloging-in-Publication Data
dePaola, Thomas Anthony.
The clown of God.
SUMMARY: A once-famous Italian juggler, now old and a
beggar, gives one final performance before a statue of Our Lady
and the Holy Child.
1. Legends—Italy. [1. Jugglers and juggling—Fiction.
2. Folklore—Italy.] I. Title.
PZ8.1.D43Cl [E] 78-3845
ISBN 0-15-219175-5
ISBN 0-15-618192-4 pb

Printed by South China Printing Co., Ltd., China

V X Z BB AA Y W U

Manufactured in China

Many, many
years ago,
in Sorrento...

there lived a small boy named Giovanni
who had no mother and no father.
He dressed in rags and begged
his bread and slept in doorways.

But he was happy, and he could do
something wonderful.

He could juggle.

Every day he would go to Signor Baptista's
fruit and vegetable stall and juggle.

He would juggle lemons
and oranges,
apples
and eggplants,
and even zucchini.

Crowds would gather to watch, and when
Giovanni had finished, they would buy from
Signor Baptista. Then Signor Baptista's wife
would give Giovanni a bowl of hot soup.

It was a very good arrangement.

One day a troupe of traveling players came to town, and Giovanni watched as Arlecchino and Colombina, in their beautiful clothes, danced and sang.

"Oh," Giovanni said to himself, "that is the life for me!"

So when the play was over, Giovanni went
and spoke to the Maestro.

"No, no," said the Maestro. "I have no need
for a ragamuffin. Go beg your bread somewhere else."

"But I could be very helpful," pleaded
Giovanni. "I could help unpack and pack up.
I could take care of the donkey. And, Maestro,"
added Giovanni, "I can *juggle!*"

"Not bad," said the Maestro, watching.
"With a bit more training and practice....
All right! But *no* money. A place to sleep,
the companionship of the finest players in Italy,
and a bowl of noodles. That's all."

"*Grazie,* Signor," said Giovanni.

"Go get your things. We leave in an hour,"
said the Maestro.

And so Giovanni said good-bye
to Signor and Signora Baptista
and became a traveling player.

Not long after, the Maestro gave him a costume and Giovanni juggled for the crowds.

He would put on a clown's face, step out from the curtain before the play began, bow, open up a colorful bag, roll out a carpet, and begin.

He would juggle sticks.

Plates.

Then he would balance the plates on the sticks
and twirl them.

He would juggle clubs,
rings,
and burning torches.

Finally he would toss a red ball and an orange ball.
Then a yellow ball.

A green, a blue, and a violet ball until it looked
as if he were juggling the rainbow.

"And now for the Sun in the Heavens!" he would cry.
Still juggling, he would pick up a shining golden ball
and toss it higher and higher, faster and faster.
And how the crowds would cheer!

Giovanni became very famous, and it wasn't
long before he said good-bye to the traveling troupe
and set off on his own.

Up and down Italy he traveled, and although
his costume became more beautiful,
he always kept the face of a clown.

Once he juggled for a duke.

Once for a prince!

And it was always the same.

First the sticks, then plates, then the clubs,
rings, and burning torches.

Finally the rainbow of colored balls.

"And now for the Sun in the Heavens," he would shout,
and the golden ball would fly higher and higher
and the crowds would laugh and clap and cheer.

One day, between two towns, Giovanni was sitting in the shade of a tree, eating a lunch of bread and cheese. Two Little Brothers came down the road.

"Will you share your food with us, good clown," they asked, "for the love of God and the blessings of our Brother Francis?"

"Sit down, good fellows," Giovanni said. "There is more than enough."

As the three men ate, the two Little Brothers told Giovanni how they went from town to town, begging their food and spreading the joy of God.

"Our founder, Brother Francis, says that everything sings of the glory of God. Why, even your juggling," said one of the brothers.

"That's well and good for men like you, but I only juggle to make people laugh and applaud," Giovanni said.

"It's the same thing," the brothers said. "If you give happiness to people, you give glory to God as well."

"If you say so!" said Giovanni, laughing. "But now I must be off to the next town. *Arrivederci,* good brothers—and good luck!"

And wherever Giovanni went, the air
was filled with his flying sticks and plates,
his clubs and rings and torches.
And, always, his rainbow of balls and
"the Sun in the Heavens."

And wherever Giovanni went,
the faces of the crowds would be all
smiles, and the sound of laughter and
cheers would ring through the towns.

Years passed.

Giovanni grew old and times became hard.

People no longer stopped to watch.
"It's only the old clown who juggles things.
We've all seen him before," they said.

Giovanni was sad, but still he juggled
until one day he *dropped* "the Sun in
the Heavens," and the rainbow of balls
came crashing down and the crowd
stood around him and laughed!
But not from joy.

Then they did a terrible thing.
They threw vegetables and stones at
Giovanni, so that he had to run for his life.

Beside a stream, Giovanni took off his clown face.
He put away his sticks and his plates,
his clubs and rings and colored balls.
He put away his costume,
and he gave up juggling forever.

What little money he had soon was gone, and his clothes became rags and he begged his bread and slept in doorways as he had done as a child.

"It's time to go home," the old man said wearily. And he headed back to Sorrento.

It was a cold winter night when he finally arrived.

The wind blew hard, and an icy rain was falling.

Up ahead loomed the monastery church of the Little Brothers.

The windows were in darkness.

Wet and cold, old Giovanni crept inside
and fell in a heap in a corner.

Soon he was asleep.

It was the music that woke him up.
The church was blazing with candlelight
and filled with people, singing, "Gloria! Gloria!"

Giovanni could scarcely believe his eyes. So
much *beauty*. A long procession of brothers,
priests, sisters, and townspeople, all carrying
beautiful gifts, was winding its way through
the church.

They placed their gifts in front of a statue—
of a lady and her child.

"What is all this?" asked old Giovanni
of someone standing near.

"Why, old man, it's the birthday
of the Holy Child," the woman said.
"It's the procession of the gifts."

Giovanni watched in amazement until the singing was over. Then the church emptied of all the people and was darkened except for the bright candles surrounding the Lady and the Child.

Giovanni moved closer. The Child in the Lady's arms seemed so serious, so stern.

"Oh, Lady," said Giovanni. "I wish I had something to offer, too. Your child seems so sad, even with all these beautiful gifts. But wait—I used to make people smile."

Giovanni opened his bag and shook
out his old costume. Then he put on
his clown face, bowed, rolled out the
little rug, and began to juggle.

First the sticks.

Then the plates.

Next he twirled the plates on the
sticks.

And then the clubs and rings…

The Brother Sexton, who was coming in to lock the doors, saw Giovanni juggling. He was horrified.

"Father Master," he cried, rushing off to get the priest.

"A sacrilege. Come quickly!"

But Giovanni didn't hear or notice him.

"And now," said Giovanni, smiling at the face
of the Child, "First the red ball, then the orange…

"Next the yellow...

"And the green, blue, and violet."

Around and up they went
until they looked like a rainbow.

"And finally," cried Giovanni, "*the Sun in the Heavens!*"
The gold ball flew up and around and around, higher and higher.
Giovanni had never juggled so well in all his life.

Higher and higher, faster and faster. A blaze of color filled the air. It was magnificent!

Giovanni's heart was pounding.

"For You, sweet Child, for You!" he cried.

Then suddenly, his old heart stopped.
And Giovanni fell dead to the floor.

The priest and Brother Sexton came rushing
in. Stooping over old Giovanni, the priest
said, "Why, the poor clown is dead.
May his soul rest in peace."

But the Brother Sexton backed away, and with
his mouth wide open, he stared at the statue
of the Lady and her Holy Child.
"Oh, Father," he said, pointing. "Oh, Father, look!"

The Child was smiling,
and in His hand He held the golden ball.

Drawing upon his heritage, his fine arts background, and his personal religious experience (he once entered an order of brothers), TOMIE DEPAOLA has carefully and patiently researched, both here and abroad, every detail of his paintings for his rendition of *The Clown of God*. He has set the story at the beginning of the Renaissance — the time the legend was thought to have originated — and painstakingly reproduced the scenery, clothing, and customs of that period. The statue of the Madonna and Child, however, comes from the earlier, more primitive Sienese school of art, since Mr. dePaola felt that "surely such a piece would have been an older, greatly revered carving." But even if such devoted attention to the accuracy of this work were not taken into account, the sheer beauty and design of the artist's renderings cannot fail to impress even the most casual viewer.

Internationally known for his work in children's books, Mr. dePaola makes his home in New Hampshire.

The book was set in 14-pt. Trump Medieval by Frost Bros.

The drawings were done in pencil, ink, and watercolor on Fabriano 140-lb. handmade watercolor paper.
Color separations by Offset Separations/Mondadori, Verona, Italy
Printed by South China Printing Co., Ltd., China
Book design by Kay Lee